Be helpful

We have fun!

We care about each other

Share happy cupcakes

I give great hugs

I'm here for you

Best friends forever!

For Andrew, my best friend forever — C.H.

To my lovely friends from JMHS,
Ledbury 1982-1987 — A.P.

First edition for the United States and Canada published

in 2019 by B.E.S. Publishing
First published in 2019 by Scholastic Children's Books

Text copyright © Caryl Hart, 2019

Illustration copyright © Ali Pye, 2019

The moral rights of Caryl Hart and Ali Pye have been asserted.

ISBN: 978-1-4380-5076-8

Library of Congress Control No.: 2018966463

Date of Manufacture: May 2019
Manufactured by: Tien Wah Press, Johor, Malaysia

Printed in Malaysia
9 8 7 6 5 4 3 2 1

All inquiries should be addressed to:
B.E.S. Publishing
250 Wireless Boulevard
Hauppauge, New York 11788
www.bes-publishing.com

TOGETHER WE CAN!

CARYL HART

B.E.S.
PUBLISHING

ALI PYE

A friend is a buddy, a pal, or a mate,
a person who's special, who makes you feel great.

They're fun to hang out with, at home, school, or play.
They're there when you need them ...

They cheer up your day!

A friend might help out
when your class work
is **tricky**,

or scratch your right ear
if your hands
are **all sticky!**

At school you might sit
with a new friend for lunch,
and share your snacks with a loud

munch,

crunch,

crunch!

At playtime, a friend will take turns on the slide,

or count up to ten, when it's your turn to hide.

Our friends are all different, but one thing is true—

Each one is quite precious, and that includes

YOU!

All over the world and from since time began,
we show every day that...
together we CAN!

Some friends look the same,
like these two little boys,
they both have short hair
and they like the same toys.

But friends can be different and still get along.
There aren't any rules.
There is no right or wrong.

Some friends
speak a language
we don't understand.

They still laugh
together,

and walk hand in hand.

Some people need gadgets to help them have FUN!

Whatever they use, they're great friends,
each and every one!

Some people have one friend
and others have many.
Perhaps you know someone who doesn't have any?

If someone is lonely,
there's **lots** you can do.
To make them feel better, just BE a friend, too!

All over the world
and from since time began,

we show every day that...

...together we CAN!

Some friends are nearby,
they can play every day.

While others are distant—
they live far away.

All over the globe,
there are people who care.

Just look and you'll see,

there are friends

everywhere!

We meet brand new people wherever we go.

Look, here are some friends who you might not yet know!

A friend can have six legs...

...or four legs...

...or two!

What kind of a friend is the best one for YOU?

All over the world
and from since time began,
we show every day that...

...together we CAN!

If YOU want a friend,
here's a thing you should know:

We MAKE friends, it's easy!
Just give it a go.

Find someone you like,
and just ask them their name.

Invite them to lunch, or to join in your game.

If someone is sad,
you could give them a cuddle,

or help them get out
of a difficult muddle!

Try baking some cupcakes,
or make a nice card.

Great
FrIEND
Award.

See? Making a friend
really isn't too hard.

A good friend like you
forgives any mistakes.
When YOU'RE wrong, say: "Sorry,"
with hugs or handshakes.

A nice friend like you
will be happy to share.

You'll listen and make others
feel that you care.

All over the world
and from since time began,
we show every day that...

...together we CAN!

By making new friends, we can all come together.
Be loving and kind and you'll have friends forever.

Smile!

Feelings are important

I'll hold your hand

Let's be friends

I'm good at sharing

Be gentle

Spread the love

Hugs!